The Man
on the Unicycle
and Other Stories
Elizabeth Bram

Elizabeth Bram

Greenwillow Books

A Division of William Morrow & Company, Inc., New York

TO SUSAN AND PEGGY

10 9 8 7 6 5 4 3 2 1

Library of Congress Cataloging in Publication Data
Bram, Elizabeth. The man on the unicycle and other stories.
(Greenwillow read-alone)   Contents: The tiger hunt. —
The man on the unicycle. — The balloon party.
[1. Short stories] I. Title. PZ7.B7357Man [Fic] 76-22666
ISBN 0-688-80059-9   ISBN 0-688-84059-0 lib. bdg.

Contents

The Tiger Hunt

It was a bright and sunny day.

Karen and Freddy

were going tiger hunting.

They started off

down the block.

They had a bag of fruit

and sandwiches for lunch.

They passed Mrs. Brown's house.
She was sitting on the front porch
with several of her ten cats.
"Where are you going?"
asked Mrs. Brown.
"We are going tiger hunting,"
said Karen.

"I have just the thing for you
to take along," said Mrs. Brown.
She went into her house
and brought out a book of poems.
"Be sure and stop by later
and tell me what happens,"
said Mrs. Brown.

Karen and Freddy went on
down the block with the bag
of food and the book of poems.
Soon they were in front
of Mr. Hubbard's house.
He was raking leaves.

"Where are you two going
in such a hurry?" said Mr. Hubbard.

"We are going to catch a tiger,"
said Karen.

"Well, in that case, you will need
something to catch him in."

Mr. Hubbard went into the garage.

He came back with a large paper bag.

The children thanked Mr. Hubbard.

They went on down the block

with the bag of food,

the book of poems,

and the paper bag.

Just as they reached the woods,

George Murphy the milkman

stopped to talk with them.

"Where are you going?" he said.

"We are going to catch a tiger."

"Here's something you can use,"
said George.
He gave them a bottle of milk
and a paper cup to put it in.
"All cats like milk," he said,
"and the tiger is part
of the cat family."

Karen and Freddy thanked the milkman
and went on into the woods.

They walked for a while until
they found just the right place.
They opened up the paper bag
and poured some milk into the cup.
"We'll have to wait a while
before the tiger comes," said Karen.

They went and sat down
by a little stream to have lunch.
Karen took out the book of poems
and began to read aloud.

After Karen had read
all the poems in the book,
they tiptoed back to the bag.
They looked inside.
A very small tiger
was curled up in the bag.

Freddy carried the tiger.

Karen read poems to him

as they walked home

through the woods.

They knocked on Mrs. Brown's door.

Good smells were coming

from the kitchen.

When Mrs. Brown came to the door,

Freddy showed her the tiger

that they had found.

"Oh, Julius," said Mrs. Brown,

"I've been looking all over for you."

"Come on in,"

she said to the children.

"You're just in time for

some freshly baked cookies."

The children went in and sat down.
They had cookies and talked
about catching the tiger.

When it was time to go home,

Karen handed Mrs. Brown

the book of poems.

"I'd like you to keep it,"

said Mrs. Brown.

"Thank you for bringing Julius home."

The Man
on the Unicycle

Freddy was playing alone
in his yard one day.
A man on a unicycle rode by.
"The circus is over," he said,
"but you can come and visit
if you like."

Freddy followed the man
on the unicycle.
They came to a huge field
where the circus had been.

There was no one
riding on the carrousel,
and all the circus animals were
grazing in the field.

The acrobats
were hanging
from a tree.

26

The fat man
was drinking tea.
"I'm too fat," he said.
"It's time to go
on a diet."

The thin man was eating bananas.

"Time to fatten up," he said.

The bareback rider
was getting on her horse.
"Where are you going?"
asked Freddy.

"I'm going down to the lake,"
she said, and rode off.

The lion tamer came by.

"We are all going swimming,"

he said.

"Would you like to come?"

So Freddy went down to the lake
and went swimming with
all the circus people and animals.

33

Later, they sat on the shore

and built a bonfire and sang songs.

The circus musicians played music.

Everyone danced.

36

Then the man on the unicycle rode up
and said it was time to go.

Freddy waved good-bye,

and he and the man on the unicycle

started home.

The Balloon Party

A man on the corner
was selling balloons.

Karen bought one
for herself,
one for her mother,
one for her father,
and one for
her stuffed rabbit.

When she got home, she found that
her mother had bought a balloon too.
It was tied to the arm of a chair.

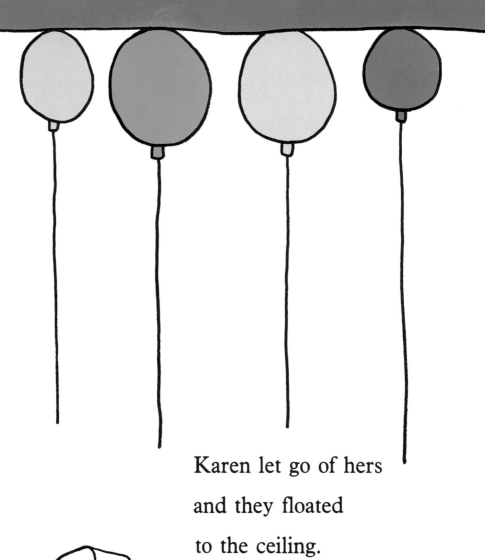

Karen let go of hers
and they floated
to the ceiling.

Soon her father came in.

He was carrying three more balloons.

"It looks like a party," he said.

He began tying the balloons down
around the room.

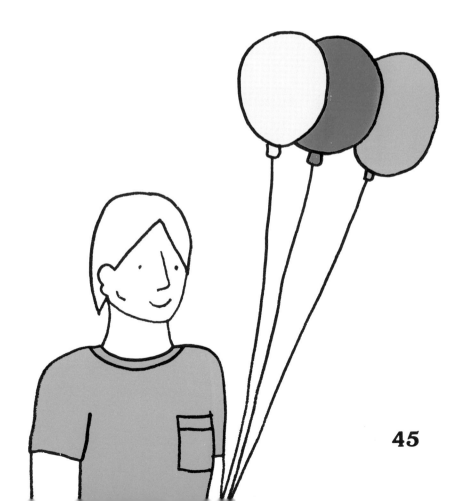

Karen's friend Freddy walked in.

He was carrying a balloon too.

Soon all the children
on the block arrived.
Word had spread that Karen
was having a balloon party.

There were balloons everywhere.

The living room was full.

The children were having
so much fun with the balloons
that they stayed past dinner time.
Their parents came to look for them.
When they saw the balloon party,
they wanted to join in too.

The balloon man was still on the corner.

So they all went out

and came back with balloons.

Karen began carrying balloons
into the bathroom,
where they hung from the ceiling
and filled up the bathtub.

There were balloons all over the kitchen.

Karen carried some
down to the basement.

Soon there was no more room
in the house.

So all the children
and their parents
went outside
and watched the sunset.

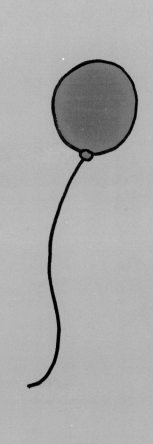